FOR ALL OUR BABIES!

Jaye, Merlin, Finn, Sorley,
Loki & Poppy

First published in the United States 1998 by

Little Tiger Press

N16 W23390 Stoneridge Drive, Waukesha, WI 53188

Originally published in Great Britain 1998 by

Levinson Children's Books, London

Text copyright © Tony Bonning 1998

Illustrations copyright © Sally Hobson 1998

CIP Data is available

Printed in Belgium

First American Edition

ISBN 1-888444-43-6

1 3 5 7 9 10 8 6 4 2

Another Fine Mess

by
Tony Bonning
Pictures by
Sally Hobson

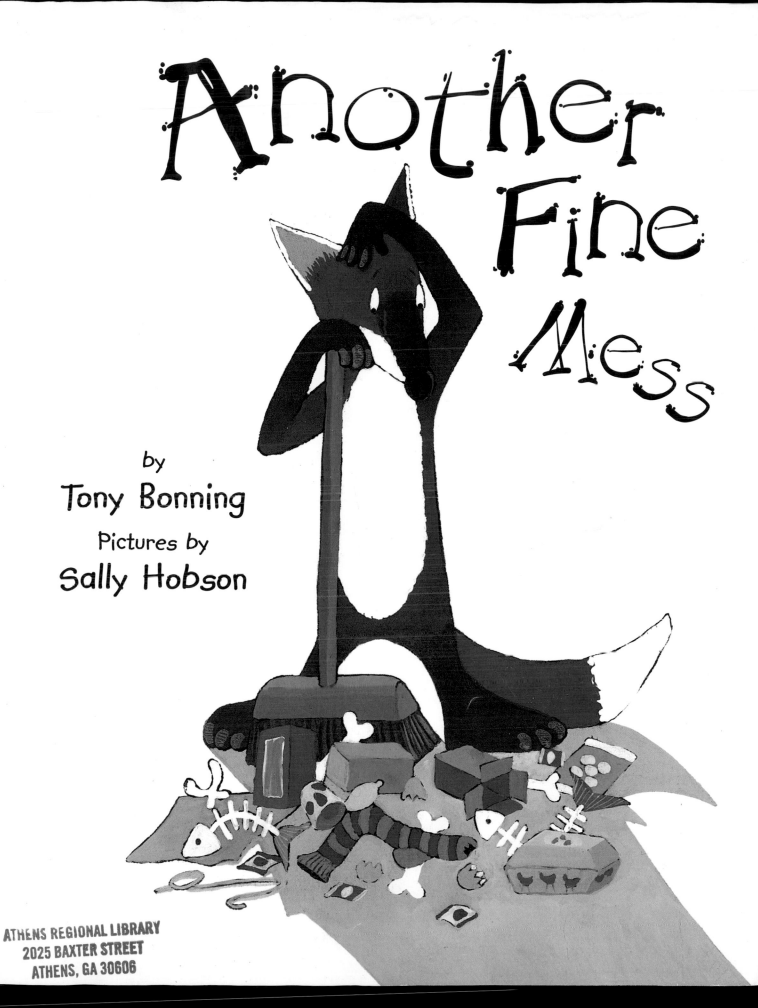

Early one morning there was
a knock on Fox's door.
"Special delivery!"
called a squeaky voice.
Fox had been out all night,
and his eyes were still half-closed.
He opened the door and yawned,
and a letter was thrust under
his nose.
"Thanks," he said sleepily,
trudging back to bed.

Fox switched on the lamp and snuggled down under the covers to read the letter, which said:

Dear Nephew,
I will pay you a visit
on the next full moon.
Sincerely,
Uncle Ferdinand

Fox looked at his calendar. "Oh no!" he cried. "The next full moon is tonight! Oh dear!" he wailed. "My den is a mess!"

Fox took out his broom and swept the whole house,
until there was a big pile of trash at the front door.
Where shall I put it now? he wondered.
He decided to push it outside. As Fox swept
the trash along the path that ran around
the hill, he noticed a hole in the ground.

"This will do just fine," he said, sweeping the trash down the hole. Then Fox went back to his den to wait for Uncle Ferdinand.

In the meantime,
Badger woke to a
terrible CRASH!
It sounded as if the roof
had fallen in.
She jumped out of bed,
and there in the middle
of the living room was
a pile of trash!

Badger was furious.
"How did that mess get here?" she cried.
Badger fetched a broom and swept the trash out of her home, through the woods, and into a deep hole.

"In you go," she said as the trash tumbled out of sight.

The Rabbit family was just about to have some salad for lunch when the trash fell SPLAT! right in the middle of the kitchen table.
They were horrified.

"Yuck! What a mess!" said the children.
"My poor lettuce!" said Mommy Rabbit.
"Grab a brush, everyone!"
said Daddy Rabbit.

Together the family brushed
the trash off the table, out of their
burrow, and around the hill.
    They found a thick clump of grass
to hide it in, and then they all went
home to make a second lunch.

Soon after, Partridge finished pecking in the woods for her lunch and returned to the new nest she had built.

She was terribly upset to find that someone had dumped all their trash on top of it.

"What a mess!" she screeched. "How will I ever clean this up?"

Partridge gathered some
twigs to sweep the trash away
from her nest.
Finding a hole close by,
she swept the trash into it.
Then she went back to her
nest to lay some eggs.

Mole was scurrying through his house when the pile of trash fell THUMP! right on top of his head.

"Oh goodness me! Goodness me!
What is this?" he said, removing
a box from his snout.
A few sniffs told him it was
a pile of trash.
"I can't have this mess in here,"
he said, pushing it through
his tunnel under the hill.
When Mole reached his front
door, he shoved the trash
outside. Then he went indoors
to wash his paws.

Meanwhile, all the
trash rolled down the
hill and landed with a
CLATTER!
BANG!
CRASH!
right at the feet of Uncle
Ferdinand, who was on
his way to see Fox.

"What a mess!" he
said, shaking his head
and picking up the trash.
When he reached Fox's den,
he put it down outside.
"Look at this trash I found on
the road!" said Uncle Ferdinand crossly
when Fox answered the door.

"Oh no!" wailed Fox, realizing his own trash was back on his doorstep. He was about to suggest putting it back down the hole he had found earlier, when the Mouse family passed by.

"What wonderful treasures!" exclaimed Mrs. Mouse. "Do they belong to you?"

"Help yourself," said Fox with a sigh of relief as he led Uncle Ferdinand into his home.

"I wish all my
nephews were as
neat and clean as you,"
said Uncle Ferdinand,
proudly looking around the den.
"I do my best!" said Fox
with a sly grin.